MEG'S EGGS

by Helen Nicoll
and Jan Pieńkowski

PUFFIN BOOKS

It was suppertime, so Meg got out her cauldron

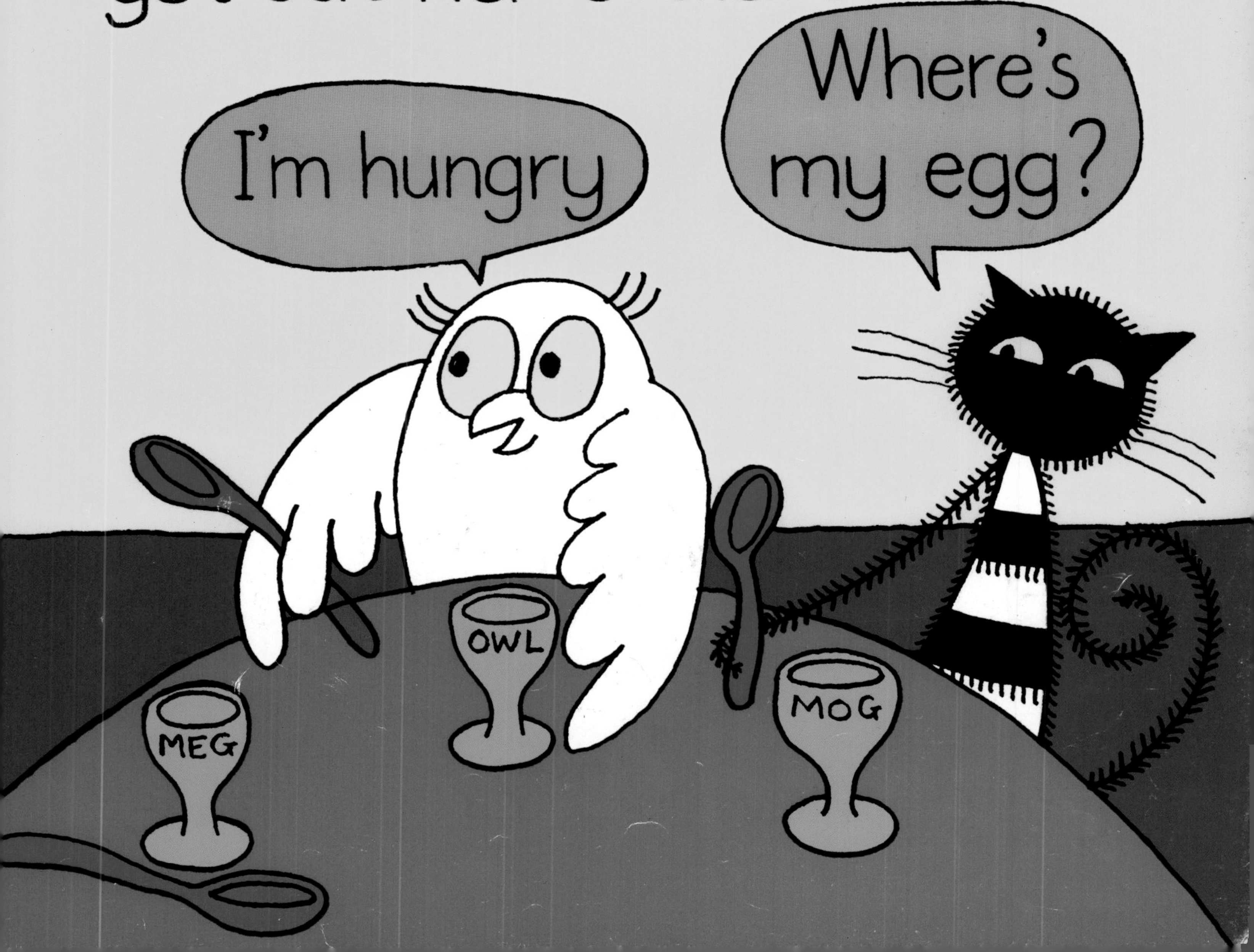

She
put
in

lizards, newts, 2 green frogs

They could not break the eggs

In the
middle
of the
night
Meg
heard

Meg's egg was hatching

Meg took Diplodocus to

the pond

Diplodocus was very happy

Mog was sleeping by his egg

BUMP THUMP

when he heard a noise

Mog
took
Stegosaurus
into
the
garden

Owl
was
watching
the
last
egg

TAP TAP

Out
jumped
Tyrannosaurus,
the
most
ferocious
of
all
the
dinosaurs

They
were
very
frightened

Tyrannosaurus
wanted
to
eat
them
all

Meg flew home and tried
to make a good spell

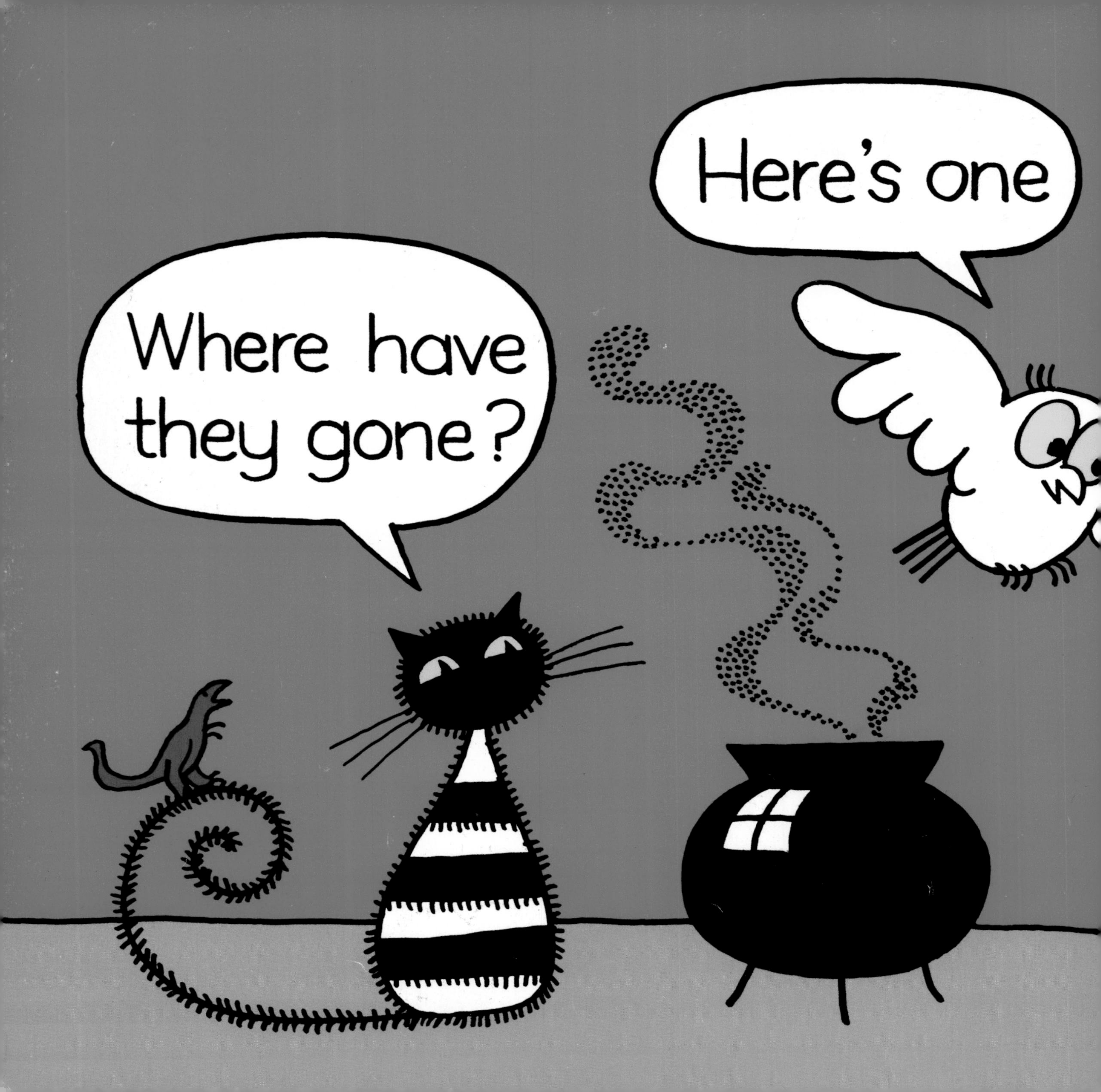
Where have they gone?
Here's one

Goodbye!

for Tom

MOG in the FOG

by Helen Nicoll
and Jan Pieńkowski

PUFFIN BOOKS

highest mountain in the world

A Sherpa saw them land

Tsing took them to a cave

The sun
came out.
It was
dazzling

Mog found some footprints

A huge cloud came down

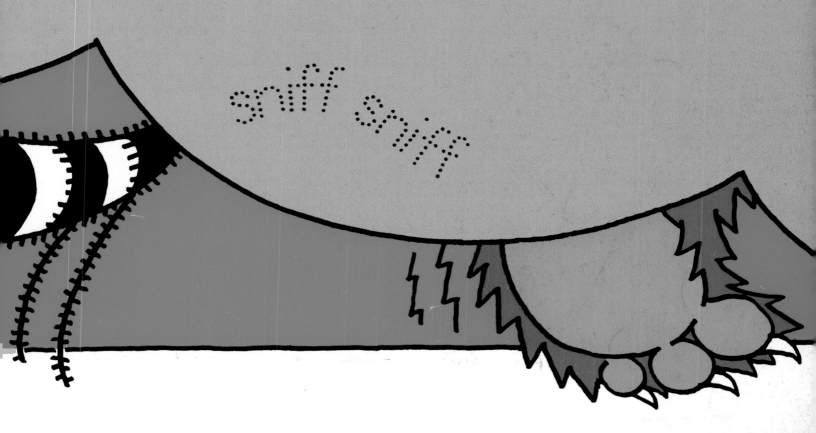

They were lost in the fog

Stay where you are!

I must just find Mog

The fog started to lift

They all ran

and
did
not
stop
until
the
top

Goodbye!

for Hannah

MEG at SEA

by Helen Nicoll
and Jan Pieńkowski

PUFFIN BOOKS

Meg, Mog and Owl

went to
the seaside

They went out in a boat

but there was no wind

The wind blew

and they swam to land

It
was
an
island

They were cold,

wet and hungry

Mog and Owl
went
fishing

They took the fish to Meg

Meg
made
smoke
signals
with
her
cloak

and took them back home

Goodbye!